# THE GREAT CANDY LAND

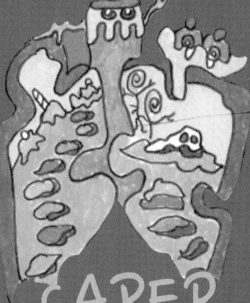

# CAPER

written by Laura Hill,

Ava Timpanaro and Kayla Timpanaro

GSWMU #5

*This book is dedicated to everyone who loves candy and a sweet little dog with a curly tail named Buster.*

ISBN-13: 978-1492925866

ISBN-10: 1492925861

# THE GREAT CANDY LAND

# CAPER

written by Laura Hill,

Ava Timpanaro and Kayla Timpanaro

GSWMU #5

To Matthew —
Get ready for a
super sweet adventure
Hi-yah!

3

The Great Story World Mix-Up
Just Got Sweeter...

Penelope and Jilly are off to Candy Land on a super sweet adventure. But their plans turn bitter when an Evil Wizard casts a rotten spell turning all the Candy Land candy sour.

Penelope and Jilly have just hours to undo the spell and make Candy Land sweet again.  But it won't be easy.  The secret to the spell is written on a golden ball that's been swallowed by a frog that is hopping down the most dangerous path in Candy Land to the Bittersweet, Dark Forest.

Find out what happens in...

**The Great
Candy Land Caper**

# Contents

# Disaster

Jilly danced up the steps to the old library twirling on her toes. She had just come from a birthday party and still wore her party dress. A blue, polka-dotted party hat was perched on her head and candy kisses were spilling out of the goody bag she clenched in her fist. She stopped for a moment to stuff a bit of chocolate in her mouth savoring the sweet flavor. A tingling feeling raced from the ends of her toes to the top of her head and she began to smile. Then she began to giggle. She giggled until she was laughing so hard that she sat down on the steps with a *whump*.

"What's so funny?" asked Penelope, who had been waiting at the top of the steps by the library door. She walked down and sat next to her sister, picking a fallen chocolate kiss off the step and popping it into her mouth.

"Hey that's mine!" said Jilly.

"You can havth it ifth you wanth it!" Penelope replied opening her mouth. Dark chocolate glistened on her tongue and teeth.

Jilly scrunched her nose and turned away. She spied another kiss on the steps, peeled off the shiny silver foil and popped it into her mouth. That delicious tingling feeling filled her up again. She felt like she could fly and rose up on her toes twirling on the edge of the step. "Look at me!" she sang, raising her hands in a graceful arc. She slid her toe up to her knee and started to pirouette, then she began to wobble. Her foot slipped and Jilly flailed her arms trying to regain her balance as she tottered on the edge of the step.

"Hold on!" cried Penelope jumping to her feet. She grabbed the bow at the back of Jilly's dress just as she started to fall. The bow unraveled and the satin slipped through her fingers, but Penelope held on tight. There was a jerk and a tearing of threads. Jilly hung suspended in mid-fall, one foot on the edge of the step, the rest of her dangling in space. Then the bow split, pulling off the fabric with a long low, *ripppppp.*

Penelope pulled as hard as she could. She fell backwards onto the step, the torn bow lying limp in her fingers. Jilly tumbled onto her lap with an, *oof.* As the girls untangled themselves the sky grew dark. Penelope narrowed her eyes and studied the clouds. As she did a big drop of rain fell hitting her *smack* in the middle of her forehead.

"Come on," she said, pulling Jilly up as she stood.

Several more raindrops plopped on her head, spotting the ground with large wet rings and soaking into the dark fabric of her jeans. In a few minutes it was going to pour. Penelope ran up the steps two at a time and flung the door open. Thunder cracked. She ducked into the library just as the rain came down in sheets. But where was Jilly? Penelope could see her sister out on the library steps scooping up wet candy and putting it into her goody bag, her ponytails dripping like a faucet, her dress plastered to the back of her legs.

"Jilly, what are you doing?"

"I'm getting my candy kisses."

"You're getting soaked!"

"No I'm not!" Jilly replied, plucking a chocolate off the steps and dropping it into her bag. She stuck out her chin defiantly. Jilly could be so stubborn! Penelope huffed and stomped down the steps. By the time she reached Jilly she was sopping wet, too.

"Don't you think you've had enough candy?" she said taking the goody bag from Jilly's hand. "You're going to get sick!" Jilly snatched it back spilling the chocolate all over the steps again. She stooped, pushing them back into her goody bag, the rain and chocolate mixing together in a dripping mess.

"Just leave them," said Penelope, pulling Jilly toward the door. But Jilly stuck out her chin and dug in her heels. "Look, if you come now, you can have some of my gumballs when we get home."

"The ones from the big spiral gumball machine, the one that plays music?"

"Yes," said Penelope.

"How many?"

"One."

"Five."

"Two."

"Three."

"Fine, *three*, can we just go inside!"

Jilly smiled and walked through the door. She smoothed out the folds of her party dress and shook her wet hair splattering tiny drops of rain across the wall. "Look its raining inside!" she giggled.

But Penelope was not in a giggling mood. When Mom had dropped them off she had put Penelope in charge and Mom wouldn't be happy to see Jilly soaking wet and covered in chocolate. "Let's go to the children's room and get warmed up," she said.

Penelope had just turned eleven and was not eager spend the rest of the afternoon in the children's room. But Jilly was only eight and she loved to set up all the stuffed animals and read books to them. Besides the children's room was always noisy and bright and Penelope did like to build with the Legos they had there.

But Jilly had other ideas. Instead of heading to the children's room she plopped herself down in a big chair by the circulation desk. The chair was covered in dark brown leather and had tall wingbacks that towered high over Jilly's head. It was so big her feet stuck off the edge. She plopped her soggy goody bag down in her lap and peeled the wrapper off a mushy chocolate kiss.

Ms. Valentine, the head librarian, was checking out books at the circulation desk, her tight bun bobbing up and down as she scanned the bar codes on the back of the book jackets. A tired looking mom stood at the desk holding the hand of a little boy who was sucking loudly on four of his fingers while he stuck his thumb up the side of his nose. He watched with interest, sucking harder, as Jilly dropped the chocolate kiss wrapper onto the floor and popped the candy into her mouth, smacking her lips loudly as she ate it.

Ms. Valentine's bun stopped bobbing. She looked up then snapped her head right then left, her trained eye scanning the library foyer for the noisy lip smacker. Then she looked right at Jilly. Jilly clamped her mouth shut. She covered the goody bag in her lap with her hands. Then she reached down and kicked the candy wrapper under the chair with her toe. Ms. Valentine narrowed her eyes. "Shhh," she said putting a finger to her lips and went back to checking out books.

The boy at the circulation desk took his

fingers out of his mouth. "I want candy too!" he pouted.

"I'm sorry," said Ms. Valentine, shaking her head, "but there is no candy allowed in the library." She handed him a bookmark instead. He turned it over in his hand and frowned.

When she was sure Ms. Valentine wasn't looking Jilly unwrapped another kiss and popped it into her mouth. As the creamy chocolate melted on her tongue her mouth began to tingle, then her fingers and her toes. She felt like she could bounce out of her chair, right over Penelope's head, over the circulation desk right past the little boy who was now crying and stamping his feet.

"But she has candy!" he said, pointing at Jilly.

Jilly froze in mid-chew. Ms. Valentine was frowning in her direction. There was no hiding, she had been caught red-handed. A ring of chocolate circled her lips and a shiny silver candy wrapper lay in her lap. Ms. Valentine came out from behind the circulation desk, her square heels clacking loudly across the wooden floor.

"Run!" cried Jilly, grabbing Penelope's hand, her goody bag clenched in the other.

She dragged Penelope through the library running as fast as she could, Ms. Valentine and her clacking heels following close behind. She was calling for them to stop, "Girls!"

Penelope tripped behind Jilly bumping into books and patrons as she went. They ran through the children's room. "Watch it!" cried an irritated clerk as she tried to steady a huge stack of picture books. They fell to the floor with a crash. Ms. Valentine clacked quickly past and the clerk joined the chase.

"Give me the goody bag and we'll throw it away, then Ms. Valentine will stop chasing us!" whispered Penelope.

"Never!" Jilly cried, skidding around a corner.

She dragged Penelope through the teen center past a large screen where a bunch of boys were playing video games. "I got you now," a big boy grinned, working his controller. The image on the screen faded in and out then flickered off as the girls ran past.

"Hey!" he cried, scowling at Penelope. She shrugged and stumbled behind Jilly. Ms. Valentine clacked by with the children's room clerk hurrying after her. The boys from the teen center lumbered after them, joining the chase. Jilly pulled Penelope into the *quiet room* where an old man with a red cap was playing chess.

"Checkmate," he said moving his rook. Penelope caught the edge of the board as she ran past sending chess pieces flying in the air.

"Hey!" the man cried.

"Sorry," Penelope called over her shoulder, but she didn't stop running, she just had to get that goody bag away from Jilly!

Ms. Valentine's heels clacked louder and faster behind them, click *clack, click clack*. The clerk hurried behind her and the boys from the teen center lumbered along. The old men playing chess wobbled up on their canes and joined the chase tapping the ground as they hobbled after Penelope and Jilly.

Now Ms. Valentine, the children's room clerk, the boys from the teen center and the old men playing chess were chasing them. Penelope pulled her hand free of Jilly's and grabbed her shoulder spinning her around. She pulled the goody bag out of Jilly's hand.

"I know you have a sweet tooth," she gasped, "but we can't get kicked out of the library because of it. Mom will kill us!"

"You mean she'll kill *you*, she put you in charge. Besides I'm not the one with the sweet tooth, you are!" Jilly puffed and grabbed for the bag.

Penelope pushed past Jilly. Up ahead was a long dark corridor. "Come on," she cried racing past the stacks of books. The corridor grew dimmer as she ran and Penelope could glimpse the titles of ancient looking books, *The Frog Prince* and *Funky Weather Experiments to Amaze Your Friends*. She ran until she could no longer hear the clacking of Ms. Valentine's shoes or the hurrying clerk or the lumbering boys or the tapping of the old men's walking sticks. In fact she couldn't hear anything at all except her own panting breath and the rain pattering on the rooftop.

Penelope slowed down. She was deep in the corridor in a part of the library she had never seen before. Her heart pounded and her breath came in ragged gasps. The sweet tooth Jilly had referred to throbbed, it was not a sweet tooth, it was Penelope's first cavity. But where was Jilly? Penelope strained to see in the dim light. Jilly was nowhere in sight!

"Jilly," she called out softly. Her heart raced anew. What if Ms. Valentine had caught Jilly while Penelope ran ahead? What if she had Jilly in her office right now and was calling Mom! "Jilly," she called out again peering through the gloom for a sign of her sister.

"Hi-yah!"

A loud cry pierced the stillness. From the shadows sprang Jilly karate chopping her hands wildly as she crashed into Penelope. The goody bag fell to the floor and Jilly scooped it up. The loud clack of Ms. Valentine's heels echoed down the corridor. Jilly tuned to the wall, a wild look in her eyes.

"Hi-yah," she cried hitting the wall with the side of her hand.

A white light appeared. It began to shimmer, shining dimly at first then growing brighter as it raced across the wall, turning at sharp angles until it had formed several boxes surrounded by a large rectangle. It looked like a giant candy bar with a knob in the center, it looked like the secret door! Jilly reached out and grasped the knob with both hands turning it then pushing with all her might. The door swung open. Bright light streamed out from inside.

"Wow," Jilly whispered, stepping into the light. The door began to shimmer. "Wait for me!" cried Penelope, scrambling through. The door closed behind them with a click fading into the wall, leaving a confused Ms. Valentine standing in the corridor, staring in disbelief.

# The Chocolate Sea

Jilly rubbed her eyes. As the bright light cleared and the room came into focus her heart began to pound. She was standing in the secret room at the library where the map of Story World was hidden. She and Penelope had discovered it by accident several weeks ago, but today something was very different. Today the room was packed from floor to ceiling with candy.

Jilly ran up to a huge mound of chocolate that had been stacked to look like a giant staircase and licked the side. She ducked under marshmallows piled into high towers that swayed from side to side, tipping until they were about to fall before springing back up again. Swedish fish swam in bowls of fizzy water, pop rocks exploded like mad, cotton candy hung from the rafters and all around were piles of sweets.

"Penelope, it's like a dream come true!" said Jilly, breathing in the delicious aroma of sugar and chocolate.

But Penelope wasn't listening. She had found a trail of puzzle pieces and was following them to a globe with the words Story World etched across the top. She ran her fingers over the outline of the Story World map then gave the globe a spin. Where they had fixed the stories puzzle pieces stuck to the globe but most of them were still lying on the floor. Penelope sighed. It was their fault the globe had broken into a million pieces and the stories had gotten mixed-up. There were so many to fix they might never get them all back together.

"Hey, look at me!" cried Jilly.

Jilly was running up the giant staircase, splashing through puddles of melted chocolate as she went. When she reached the top she plunged her hand into one of the marshmallow towers. She pulled out a fistful of fluff and stuffed it in her mouth, smiling so that it oozed out the sides. "Delicious" she muttered, sucking the fluff back in.

Then she spied the cotton candy strung across the ceiling. She climbed to the top of the marshmallow tower. It wobbled under her weight. Jilly steadied herself and when the tower stopped wobbling she reached up high, standing on her toes, but the strands of pink and blue cotton candy still fluttered just beyond her fingertips. She could practically taste the spun sugar melting in her mouth, if she could just reach a little higher!

Jilly thought for a moment. She steadied herself again, then she swung her arms and jumped with all her might. The marshmallow tower leaned to one side. "Look out!" Penelope cried, as the tower swayed then sprang back again. Jilly grabbed the strand of cotton candy, but it could not hold her, she started to fall. Her feet scraped the topmost marshmallow, wheeling, but it bounced out from underneath her toes. She grabbed hold of the tower wrapping her arms and legs around it as it bent low to the ground.

"Jump off!" yelled Penelope.

Jilly did. When she jumped the tower, having nothing to hold it back, sprang up with such force it ripped through the cotton candy strands tearing them from the ceiling one by one leaving a trail of spun sugar in its wake. It wobbled as far as it could go then came crashing back toward the girls, smashing through the chocolate stairs and scattering candies all around the room. Marshmallows, pop rocks, Swedish fish and chocolate chunks came crashing to the ground with a *splat,* and when it hit the floor, the chocolate began to melt.

"What did you do?" cried Penelope.

"I didn't do anything!" Jilly wailed.

The chocolate melted into a pool that quickly grew to the size of a pond, then as big as a lake until the floor was completely covered. It rose until it became a sea, reaching Penelope and Jilly's knees, then their waists. Penelope grabbed Jilly's hand. The only way out was the secret door, they had to get to it before the sea covered it up!

They began to swim, stroking through the thick chocolate but it weighed them down and made them slow. By the time they got to the spot in the wall where the secret door should have been, it had disappeared! Penelope dove under the chocolate, kicking until she reached the door. She pulled on the doorknob with all her might but the weight of the chocolate pressing against the secret door was too great, it was stuck fast.

She kicked to the surface and spied Jilly clinging to a marshmallow, using it as a float. The top of her head was pressed against the ceiling. It wouldn't be long before the room was completely filled with chocolate. Penelope swam over and grabbed hold of the float. When she did the marshmallow lurched and Jilly's fingers slipped off the slick round side. She lost her grip and sank into the chocolate.

The sea churned with bubbles. Penelope watched in horror as they burst to the surface, then they stopped. She stared at the spot where Jilly had been her heart racing. A moment later Jilly's hand broke through the chocolate. She dug her fingers into the marshmallow and pulled herself up sputtering, spitting out chocolate and a puzzle piece that had gotten lodged between her teeth. On it was a picture of a dark haired boy, he was holding the hand of a little girl with long braids. They were wandering through a forest that seemed to go on forever.

"That's it!" cried Penelope, hoisting Jilly up further. She grabbed the puzzle piece, "Don't you see?"

Jilly shook her head.

"If we find another puzzle piece it will take us to Story World!"

Jilly's eyes grew wide. Penelope was right. If they fit two puzzle pieces together it would take them to Story World. But they had never been able to choose which stories they would fix before, the puzzle pieces had always presented themselves, would it work? There was no time to think about it.

"Dive!" cried Penelope, taking a deep breath before disappearing under the chocolate. Jilly did the same. They swam towards the floor stroking through schools of Swedish fish towards a luminous orb that shone with wavering light. Penelope was so close she could touch it with her fingers. It was the Story World Globe! She swam to the floor searching for the puzzle pieces that were scattered at its base.

She felt along the floor finding only smooth boards then a puzzle piece twisted beneath her fingers. It leapt up and bounded past Jilly before disappearing into the chocolate. Penelope looked at her sister, Jilly's cheeks were puffed out and her eyes looked tired. She could swim after the puzzle piece but it would mean leaving Jilly behind. There was no other choice!

Penelope pointed in the direction that the puzzle piece had gone and Jilly nodded, wrapping her arms around the globe. She didn't want to swim anymore. She waited holding her breath counting the seconds, wishing she could breathe through the chocolate like the Swedish fish.

Then a hand was on her shoulder and Penelope was shaking her. Penelope had the other puzzle piece! She pushed the piece with the little boy and girl into Jilly's hand then fit her puzzle piece into it. It was a perfect match! A green light expanded until it filled the room then it exploded with a flash and they were gone.

# Candy Land

When the light faded Jilly was no longer swimming in a sea of chocolate, she was standing in the middle of a candy field. The grass glistened with sugar glaze and when she plucked a piece it melted on the tips of her fingers. She licked the end of her pinky. A warm tingle spread through her, it was the most wonderful thing she had ever tasted! She saw Penelope standing nearby alongside a path made of colored squares lined with candied flowers.

"Whee!" Jilly squealed, rolling through the grass. Sugar stuck to her hair and crunched beneath her. She rolled, watching the world turn over and over until she landed on the path by Penelope's feet. She pulled up a blade of grass. "You've got to try this, Penelope."

But instead of trying the sweet, Penelope put

her hand to her cheek. Her cavity didn't really
hurt unless she bit down on something, but still.
"No, thanks, Jilly," she said shaking her head,
"I'm trying to figure out where this path leads to."

The sun shone brightly, its rays glinting
along a path that twisted across the landscape up
to a dark forest. Here the trees grew so tall and
thick they blocked out all the brilliant light
making the path seem dark and forbidding.
Beyond the forest rose huge mountains, one with
a twin peak that shot small rocks right into the
air. They landed with a sizzle in a fizzy blue sea
barely missing a fleet of ice cream float boats
whose paper sails luffed on long spoon masts.

The row of lollipop flowers growing at the
path's edge shimmered catching Jilly's eye. A
sweet smell wafted through the air. Jilly stuck
her finger in the center of the closest one, it
tasted just like lemon meringue! The flower
shook it's leaves at her but Jilly ignored it and

stuck her finger in another flower, this one tasted like cherry blaster. She tried root beer, grape and orange cream. "This is better than my wildest dreams!" she sighed.

Jilly could feel the tingle racing to her toes. She held out her arms and spun, giggling, until

she was dizzy then she sat with a *plop* in the middle of the path. Her goody bag slipped from her pocket and slid down the row of colored squares.  It skidded to a stop on a yellow square that lit up when the bag touched it.

"Ieeeeee-ihaaaaaaaaa!"

The most awful sound filled the air.  A big green frog with a droopy mustache and an orange sombrero leapt onto the path.  He hopped onto the yellow square landing right next to Jilly's goody bag. "Viva la frog!" he croaked.  Jilly stared in horror as his long thin tongue shot out and attached its sticky end to her goody bag.

"Hey that's mine!" she cried, jumping to her feet.

The frog pulled in his tongue and the goody bag shot past Jilly's outstretched hands right into his mouth.

"Viva la frog!" he croaked again, hopping into the air and clicking his heels together. He smacked his lips and burped, then the frog bounced down the path with Jilly hot on his trail.

Penelope sighed. "Wait for me," she hollered and ran after her sister.

# Hombre Frog

Penelope raced after Jilly but it was no use. Her sister and the frog were much faster and had run so far ahead they were little specs in the distance. Her heart raced and her breath caught in her throat, it would be impossible for her to catch up. She lifted her knees like her gym teacher had shown her and swung her arms forward as she ran. Then her foot landed on a blue square. Penelope bounced into the air! Her arms swung wildly as she went *up, up, up,* into the clouds. Then with nothing to hold her there, she began to fall.

She landed on another blue square and it lit up too. Penelope bounced into the air again. She could see Jilly chasing the sombrero-wearing frog, his mustache flapping as they went over a small hill. She scrutinized the path and this time as she started to fall Penelope aimed for another blue square. When she landed she bent her knees and swung her arms forward.

Penelope sailed high into the sky. She went over the hill where she had seen Jilly and the frog disappear. She went up above the tops of the trees. Then she fell with a thud landing right next to Jilly and an angry little girl who couldn't have been more than five years old.

"Just look what you've done!" said the little girl, glaring at Jilly. The princess dress she wore was splattered with bright orange goo.

"You let the frog get away!" cried Jilly, pointing towards a well standing close by.

"Did not!"

"Did too!"

"Well, you ruined my dress," said the little girl, "you splattered it with goo when you landed!"

"Did not," said Jilly, noticing a shiny ball the little girl held in her hand. It glimmered like a jewel and made a jingling sound when she tossed it in the air. There was a spot of orange goo stuck to its curved edge.

"There," said Jilly pointing to the spot on the ball, "*you* splattered your dress while you were playing and are trying to blame me!"

The girl glanced at the ball in her hand. There *was* a tiny patch of orange goo on it that matched the goo on her dress. She shrugged and threw the ball up in the air. It sailed over Jilly's head landing on a bright orange square. The square lit up and orange goo splashed from its center splattering Jilly's hair and clothes.

"You monster!" Jilly cried, as the girl giggled.

Penelope raised her hand hiding a smile and hurried over to the well. It was a *little* funny. But Mom had put her in charge and she was trying to be responsible.  At the well was a bucket tied to a wooden crank with a rope.  Maybe they could wash the goo away with some water.  Holding onto the rope, Penelope lowered the bucket until she heard a splash.  She grasped the handle of the crank and pushed it forward, then down, then up again.  She could hear the water sloshing in the bucket, it was much heavier now that it was full.  She pushed against the crank one more time and the bucket rose over the edge of the well.

"Ieeeeee-ihaaaaaaaaa!"

The big green frog with the droopy mustache and orange sombrero jumped out of the bucket.  He landed in the middle of the orange square splattering goo all over Penelope.

"Ick," she cried letting go of the crank.  The bucket splashed back down into the water.

"Har, Har!" croaked the frog. Then he spied the golden ball and his eyes lit up. "Viva la frog!" he cried, his long tongue shooting out. It stuck to the ball. With a loud *slurp* he swallowed it. The ball landed in his belly with a jingle and a thud.

"Stop, you hombre frog!" the little girl cried out.

But it was too late. The hombre frog, along with the golden ball and Jilly's goody bag had disappeared down the well. The little girl stared after him, her hands clenched at her sides, then a big wet tear slid down her cheek. She sat hard on the ground her shoulders shaking with sobs.

"This is all our fault," Jilly whispered, kneeling down in the grass. She put her arm around the younger girl's shoulders. "Don't cry we'll get your ball back."

The girl sniffed between sobs. "It's just, it was a gift from my father," she said, nodding toward a castle that sat on a hill beyond the well. "He told me not to loss it. Daddy is going to be so mad!"

"Your dad is the king?" asked Penelope.

"Yes," the girl replied, "I'm princess Annabella but all my friends call me Annie." A loud bell began to ring. "That's the bell for lunch, I can't be late," said Princess Annie. "Will you really get my ball back?"

"I promise," said Jilly squeezing her hand. The princess sniffed then nodded and ran off towards the castle. Jilly watched until she disappeared inside. "Wow," she said, "a real live princess!" Jilly looked over at Penelope. Her arms were crossed over her chest and her face was red, she looked like she was going to explode. "What's wrong?"

Penelope threw her hands up in the air. "How could you promise Princess Annie that *we* would get her ball back? That *hombre frog* just jumped down the well with her ball in his belly and we have no idea how to get it back. Besides, her father is the king! If we don't get the ball back now he will banished us from the kingdom or worse," Penelope drew a finger across her neck in a slashing motion.

"But we can't just leave, its our fault that the frog took her ball!" said Jilly.

"How do you figure?" asked Penelope, spreading her hands out wide. "She threw her ball, the frog took it, end of story."

"The frog was here because we were chasing it.  He never would have found the ball if wasn't for us," Jilly replied.

"You mean *you,*" said Penelope, crossing her arms over her chest again.

"I guess," said Jilly, sitting down on the edge of the orange square.  It *would* be impossible to get the ball back.  Then she brightened.  They couldn't get the ball back alone but maybe they could if they had some help.

"I know what to do," Jilly smiled, "we need to find Sparky."

# Searching For Sparky

The path that had seemed so colorful and inviting before, now twisted endlessly in front of them.  Every few steps Jilly would call out to Sparky but the changeling dog didn't answer her cry.  She was starting to get worried.

"Do you think we can find our way through Story World alone?" she asked Penelope.  That was something they had never done before, Sparky had always appeared to be their guide.

"I don't know," Penelope replied.

Jilly shivered.  It was well past mid-day and the shadows on the path were growing longer.

"Sparky," she called out. The shadows seemed to quiver as she spoke. Jilly looked more closely. It wasn't the shadows that were quivering it was the path! The green square Jilly stood on lit up. It rumbled and rolled stretching itself high into the sky until it became a giant balloon. From the ground Penelope could see it was full of water.

"Jilly, jump off!"

But Jilly did not jump off. The balloon stretched even higher and she was lifted into the air. She looked over the edge. Penelope and the path seemed very far away.

Water bubbled and gurgled stretching the balloon until it was so thin Penelope could see right through it. There was something swimming inside, its webbed feet paddling the balloon's thin skin, stretching it even further, the balloon was about to break.

"Jump, Jilly, jump now!"

Jilly jumped as the balloon burst open. A geyser of water came shooting out and riding on the top was the hombre frog.

"Ieeeeee-ihaaaaaaaaa!"

Water splashed out of the hole dousing Jilly and Penelope. It washed away the goo that covered their clothes and it sprayed the flowers growing along the path. They shook their leaves at the hombre frog who landed with a jingle in their midst. He licked his lips. Then his long tongue darted out and stuck to the center of a very berry lollipop. It shot through the air into his mouth, which closed with a loud smack. "Viva la frog," he croaked, bounding up the path.

"C'mon!" Jilly said, running after him.

As he hopped the hombre frog sang a little song:

Lollipops, lollipops are so sweet,
I think they are my favorite treat.
But if you pick one make sure you,
Ask them first or they'll chase you!
*Jingle, jingle.*

*Ask them first? Chase you?* An uneasy feeling began to build in Jilly's stomach. She looked to the side of the path, the lollipop flowers swayed harmlessly in the breeze.

*Jingle, jingle.*

Princess Annie's golden ball was jingling in the hombre frog's belly. As he hopped past the lollipop flowers they started to grow. Their white stick bodies stretched high over Penelope and Jilly's heads and the swirls of flavor on their faces twisted into pointy teeth.

"Run!" Jilly cried.

Penelope and Jilly ran down the path, the giant lollipops lumbering behind them. They grabbed at Jilly's dress and caught Penelope's hair in their leafy fingers.

"They must think we picked the very berry flower without asking," said Penelope, gasping for breath. Then they heard a familiar voice.

"Quick, over here!"

# Kids In The Candy House

Crouching in the grass by the side of the path was Sparky! Jilly and Penelope ran over and hugged the little dog. "Don't mess the fur," he smiled. Then his smile turned into a frown. "There's no time to lose!"

Sparky ran across the grass to a bridge that had been cut from a slice of red licorice. The top had been shorn off forming a slick shoot that curved down and away from the path. "Come on," he barked, hopping into the chute.

They flew around bends, twisting and turning until they had left the lollipop flowers far behind. The bridge spit them out at the edge of a forest where the scent of molasses and maple sugar hung thick in the air.

"I'm afraid we've got big trouble," panted Sparky, "Candy Land is turning sour! It started a few hours ago." Penelope and Jilly exchanged a worried glance.

"We got here a few hours ago," said Jilly.

"Then this might be worse than I thought," Sparky replied. The grass at the edge of the path was starting to turn brown.

"Do you think *we* are the reason Candy Land is turning sour?" asked Penelope.

"I don't know," Sparky replied, trotting down the path, "but we are going to need some expert help to find out.  I think I know just who to ask."

"A candy maker?" guessed Jilly, hurrying to keep up.

"No, we need someone with even more candy expertise," Sparky replied, "what we need is a *candy taster*."

In a few moments they arrived at the base of an enormous tree.  It was so big Jilly couldn't reach her arms around the trunk.  The most delicious smell was wafting off its crimped bark. Jilly reached to break a piece of it off.

"I wouldn't do that, the dark maple trees are very sensitive," said Sparky. "Here we are!"

He led them around the tree to a little rope ladder.  Jilly followed the ladder up through the branches.  Her eyes grew wide.  High in the boughs sat a child-size tree house. Its walls were made of vanilla cake, Starburst candies lined the windows and the door. Skittles along with Sour Patch Kids danced in rows across the roof to a chimney made of Golden Oreos dipped in chocolate. Jilly's mouth watered.

"It's the most beautiful thing I've ever seen," she exclaimed stepping closer. She ran her fingers over the maple tree. Its trunk was solid brown sugar creased and crinkled to look like bark. She curled her fingers around a tiny piece.

"I wouldn't do that," Sparky warned.

But he was too late. Jilly broke off the bark and popped it into her mouth. It was as delicious as she thought it would be. As soon as she did a voice floated down from above.

"Nibble, nibble little mouse, whose that nibbling on my house?"

Jilly pulled her hand away. A leafy vine snaked down from the treetop and wrapped around her waist. Jilly was hoisted into the air and disappeared from sight.

"Where did she go?" cried Penelope.

"Don't worry, she'll be fine," Sparky chuckled. He perked up his ears. Music, a heavy backbeat, was floating down from the tree house above. Sparky pointed to a doorbell that had been hung next to the tree. "Go ahead."

Penelope hesitated then pushed the doorbell with her finger. A blaring alarm sounded and hot white spotlights criss-crossed the ground. A boy with dark hair slid down the ladder a boom box clenched between his teeth. He put it on the ground, pulled his hat over his eyes and pushed play.

*Boom ticka, boom ticka, boom boom boom,* blared the radio. The boy began to wave his arms and sing:

> *So you think you can come and take a slice*
> *Of our super sweet house*
> *But that's not nice!*
> *I scream, you scream*
> *No ice cream for you,*
> *If you eat people's houses*
> *They might try to eat you, yo!*

The boy spun on his heels, stuck his thumbs under his armpits and struck a pose. Penelope's mouth hung open.

"What'd ya think?" he asked, punching the music down.

Penelope was too dumbstruck to speak.

"Yeah, I'm still working on that one," he said, pushing his hat up on his forehead.

"Do you live here?" asked Penelope, pointing at the tree house.

"Of course," said the boy.

"Do you know where my sister Jilly is?" asked Penelope.

"Of course!" he replied. "She's upstairs having tea."

# Tornados And Tea

The inside of the tree house looked as yummy as the exterior and was filled with the rich aroma of freshly baked cookies. Jilly sat with a fair-haired  girl at a table that was set for tea. They were laughing and clinking their glasses together when Penelope rushed over.

"Jilly, I was so worried!"

"I told you she was a worry wart," Jilly whispered, dunking a cookie into her teacup.

"Jilly!" Penelope looked hurt.

"I'm sorry, Penelope, I was just joking," she giggled, pouring chocolate milk from a small white teapot into a flowered cup. "Won't you join us for tea?"

Penelope touched her cheek and shook her head, she didn't want to aggravate her cavity.

"Then at least sit down and meet my new friend," Jilly said, turning to the girl at her side. "What's your name anyway?"

Before she could answer a disco ball dropped from the ceiling. Color lights flashed and the ball spun sending squares of crimson and blue dancing over the sugary walls. A spotlight hit the floor and the boy jumped into it.

"Hey Gretel, give me a beat!"

"Right," said the girl sitting next to Jilly. She jumped to her feet, cupped her hands around her mouth and started a wicked beat box.

*Chchchch boom-ch-boom-ch boom-ch-boom.*

Then the boy began to rap:

*You might have heard our story,*
 *it's no lie.*
*About a witch and a candy house,*
*we happened to find.*
*One day when we were wanderin' in the woods,*
*looking for our Papa outside our neighborhood.*

The boy started to slide from side to side. Jilly jumped up and joined him clapping to the beat.

*We are the kids, we are the kids, we are the kids in the candy house.*

*So nibble, nibble little mouse,*
*Be careful not to eat the witch's house.*
*That's a place we'll never go again,*
*'Cause Hansel and Gretel are our names!*

*Boom-ch boom-chch boom-ch boom*

Jilly and Hansel slid in unison into a big finale leaping in the air before striking a pose. Jilly fist bumped Hansel wiggling her fingers as she pulled them away.

"That deserves a firecracker," she said, then ran over to where Penelope and Sparky stood watching. "What did you think?"

"Superb," said Sparky, uncurling his tail to thump it on the floor. "But I'm afraid we have less pleasant matters to attend to, look!"

Sparky led them over to the window. From up here they could see Princess Annie's castle. It looked like a little dot sitting in a meadow. But the meadow had been destroyed and the path that ran through it broken apart. Colored tiles had been scattered in every direction. What was left was a sickly looking grey. The entire countryside looked like it had gone bad.

A funnel of black air rose into the sky. It was spinning picking up everything in its path. Trees, flowers and colored squares were sucked into the twister. It was cutting through the dark maple forest, heading straight for the tree house! Where the maple trees had stood there were ugly holes and traces of sap. The tornado reached so high even the fluffy clouds were sucked inside.

As they watched the hombre frog raced by holding onto his sombrero.

"Ieeeeee-ihaaaaaaaaa!" he cried. "Hasta arriba y lejos!"

"What did he say?" asked Jilly, frowning as she watched the twister approach. She had learned about tornados in school and they scared her to death.

"He said *up, up and away,*" barked Sparky, as the ferocious wind hit the tree house.

It shook the walls and rattled the windows

blowing gaping holes in the roof. The tree house was lifted from its branch, the maple sugar tree crumbling beneath it. They were sucked into a whirling tower of wind.

Jilly grabbed the edge of the windowsill and hung on for dear life. A chocolate cow spun past mooing in confusion, little marshmallow peeps flapped their wings and pecked at the empty air. Colored tiles whizzed past. That gave Jilly an idea. She steeled herself and climbed on the windowsill the wind whipping about her hair and face.

"What are you doing?" screamed Penelope.

"Hold hands," cried Jilly, yelling into the wind. It was lifting the tree house higher towards the top of the funnel, if the twister spit them out they would come crashing down to the ground. "Sparky, which color tile makes you bounce really high?" Sparky's ears perked up, he looked to

Hansel and Gretel.

"Right, the blue ones," Gretel replied.

Jilly could see a blue tile spinning towards them from the other side of the tornado. "Get ready to jump!"

Jilly grabbed Penelope's hand, who grabbed Gretel's hand, who grabbed Hansel's hand who scooped up Sparky and held him tight to his chest. When the blue tile floated close to the window Jilly yelled, "Jump!"

They sailed from the window, landing in the center of the blue tile. It stretched down under their weight and for a split second it seemed as if they would break through.

"We're going to crash!" Penelope cried.

Jilly held her breath. The tile stretched until

she could feel the ground beneath her toes, then it sprung back catapulting them all high into the air. They shot out of the top of the tornado into the clouds and crashed into a solid wall of pink and blue fuzz where they stuck fast.

# King Dum's Cloud Kingdum

Jilly breathed in slowly, her eyes were closed, she was *listening*. The wailing wind was gone and had been replaced by silence. Nothing stirred, there was no breeze, no bird song, just silence. She wiggled her fingers. They were stuck along with the rest of her to a wall made of fluffy pink and blue clouds.

"Penelope?" she called out softly, opening her eyes. The wall of cloud by her side billowed out.

"Over here," Penelope whispered back.

Jilly pulled her head free of the cloud wall and looked down. The world was a million miles below! Her eyes swam and it seemed like everything was spinning again. She closed them for a moment then peeked to the side. She could see Penelope was stuck to the cloud wall next to her. There were two lumps further down that had to be Hansel and Gretel. She glanced to her other side careful not to look down. A curly tail was sticking out of the cloud. Jilly heard a muffled bark. At least they had all made it out of the twister.

They were in a tight spot. Jilly, Penelope and their friends were stuck to a wall of cloud with no way to get down. If they wiggled loose from the cloud they would fall, spinning for miles before they hit the ground. If they stayed where they were the clouds might break apart forming smaller clouds that couldn't support them. Jilly tried to pull her arm away from the wall and slipped down several inches.

"Don't move," said Penelope.

Jilly wiggled her fingers in the fluff.

Something was bugging her. All around was a smell that was strangely familiar. She wiggled her fingers again and the sticky cloud stuff wound around them. That was it! Jilly stuck out her tongue and the cloud melted like spun sugar. It was made entirely of cotton candy! That gave her an idea.

Jilly pressed herself back as far into the cloud as she could, then swung her arm so she

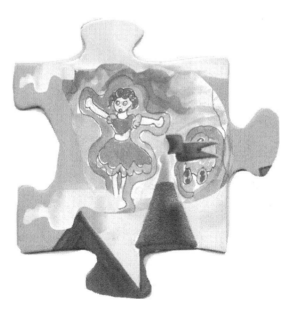

flipped over, her face buried in the cotton candy. She dug into it packing the fluff on either side until she had made a small tunnel. Sounds of people laughing and music drifted through from the other side.

"Penelope," she called, sticking her head out of the tunnel, "pull yourself free and flip over to me."

A moment later the cloud tunnel shook and Penelope flipped herself in. Jilly called out again and soon Hansel and Gretel had joined them.

"But where's Sparky?" she asked.

The cave began to quake as Sparky burst through the wall licking cotton candy off his nose with his long tongue. They hugged each other and then they all began to dig. After a few minutes they had broken through the wall.

"Whoa," said Jilly stepping into a grand courtyard.

The courtyard had been set with a circus tent that was surrounded by cloud children jetting about on bursts of hot air that made fog everywhere they went. Their parents chased after them as they wove between cloud clowns who kept bursting apart and pulling themselves back together. A troupe of acrobats had made a pyramid in front of a pair of thrones where a bored looking queen sat surrounded by an equally bored looking pack of poodles. She yawned while the little king sitting next to her clapped and clapped. They were all made entirely of clouds.

"Who is that?" asked Jilly.

"That's King Dum and this is his Cloud Kingdum," whispered Hansel. "They really are all full of hot air!"

"Right, hot heads I'd say, " piped Gretel, "it would be best if they didn't notice us."

A fluffy pink poodle sauntered up to Sparky and sniffed his nose. She began to bark running in circles. The acrobats and clowns stopped performing and the children with their parents all stared.

"Intruders!" cried the Queen, turning to the little king beside her, "well, what are you going to do about them?" The little king stopped clapping and jumped out of his seat.

"Guards, Guards, arrest them!"

From the fog rose a tall century who wore a bright helmet and held a spear, he marched towards the friends lowering his spear as he advanced. He had almost reached the little group when Hansel reached down and scooped up a handful of cloud, molding it into a ball.

"I got this," he whispered to Jilly, then turned to the guard. "Hey you!" The guard looked to both sides then pointed to himself. "Yeah you, can't you hear?" yelled Hansel.

Steam blew out of the guard's ears. He lowered his spear and charged. "They really aren't too smart," Hansel said and threw the cloud ball he had made. The guard exploded in a burst of fluff and hot air.

"Right, Hansel, don't look now," said Gretel. Slowly, Hansel turned and looked. Where the guard had stood three guards popped up from the fog.

"Everyone, make a cloud ball!" he cried, scooping up the fluff and packing it tight. Penelope, Jilly and Gretel did the same and on the count of three they threw their balls at the advancing cloud guards. The guards burst apart, hot air and fluff flying everywhere. A moment later nine guards rose from the fog.

"Again!" cried Hansel. They threw more cloud balls but each time they did the cloud guard multiplied. Soon a vast army had them surrounded. Their backs were against the massive cloud wall, there was nowhere to hide.

"Help," Jilly cried.

Next to her Sparky was changing, a trick he could do once a day, twice on special occasions. He was growing, becoming longer and rounder until he looked like a long cylinder with a huge nozzle for a mouth. He flipped a switch on his side and Sparky began to suck up the cloud army. He vacuumed up the guards, the acrobats, the clowns and the fog that covered the ground. With the fog gone Jilly could see the colored path twisting away from the courtyard.

"I have an idea!" she said, flipping Sparky's

switch. He changed back into a dog with black ears and tawny fur, a little bit fatter but no worse for the wear. Jilly spoke quickly. "Gretel, Hansel you are Candy Land experts. The colored tiles on the path, when we met Princess Annie the orange one squirted goo and when we escaped from your tree house the blue one made us jump higher. Do you know if there is a colored square that could make us change shape?"

"Why?" asked Hansel.

"The clouds can change shape, if we look like clouds we could walk right out of here," said Jilly.

"Right!" said Gretel, "The red ones make you change shape but you can't choose the shape you take."

Jilly thought a moment then her eyes grew wide. "I've got it! We can cover ourselves in this cloud stuff."

"Great idea!" said Penelope, "Since they are made out of cotton candy the clouds will stick to us and if we cover ourselves up...."

"...it won't matter what shape we take, the cloud people will think we are one of them," said Jilly.

Just then King Dum rose from his throne. His face turned grey and as he floated in the air he began to thin, spreading out until he covered the whole courtyard. He was no longer a little king he was a big angry storm cloud. Rain began to fall then hail, thunder and lightning filled the air.

"There's no time to waste!" barked Sparky scampering toward a red tile. He rolled in the clouds then jumped on top.

"Where'd he go?" asked Penelope.

"There!" said Jilly, pointing.  Floating over their heads through the storm was a fluffy little dog.  As they watched he turned into a duck, then a pizza, finally settling on a bright blue airplane.  Sparky was drifting over the wall of the cloud city changing shape as he went.  Jilly rolled through the clouds then jumped on the red square with Penelope, Hansel and Gretel right behind.  They floated over the wall, Jilly disguised as a pink unicorn, Penelope a purple owl, Hansel a boomerang and Gretel a giant donut.

King Dum chased them to the wall but his rain and hail could not reach far from his court.  They floated gently down landing at the base of a huge chocolate mountain.  The clouds that disguised them evaporated when their feet touched the ground.  They were standing next to a little wooden railroad track built along the path.  A train was clattering toward them blowing its steam whistle and playing a merry tune:

*A peanut sat on a railroad track*
*Its heart was all a-flutter*
*Along came a choo choo train*
*And whoo whoo, Peanut Butter!*

A peanut brittle train chugged up the track and stopped. The conductor leaned out his window.

"All aboard!" he yelled, looking down at the group, "that means you!"

Jilly looked at Penelope and shrugged, then they all scrambled aboard. With a loud blast from the steam whistle the train resumed chugging up the mountain, merry little songs filling the air. Soon the train was chugging at full speed and they were racing past a landscape of fudge chunks toward a white chocolate peak. They had almost reached the top when they heard a familiar cry.

"Ieeeeee-ihaaaaaaaaa!"

It was the hombre frog. "Vive la frog," he cried, as he hopped by, Princess Annie's golden ball jingled in his belly. The train began to slow down.

"What's happening, why are we stopping?" asked Penelope, sticking her head out the window as the train ground to a halt. The conductor was nowhere to be found and the chocolate that covered the mountain had turned an awful shade of grey.

"I think I know what's happening," said Jilly, looking each of her friends in the eye. "Every time the hombre frog hops by something goes wrong. I think *he* is turning Candy Land sour!"

# It's Going To Blow!

Jilly had barely finished speaking when the train started to wobble tipping from side to side on the track. She and her friends hurried towards the caboose and scrambled down a set of stairs to the ground.

The whole mountain started to shake. Jilly braced herself against a chunk of fudge and saw that Penelope was doing the same. Pop rocks were exploding everywhere chipping away pieces of the mountain with a sizzle. Slabs of chocolate slid into the fizzy sea. A chocolate mist rose from the ground.

"Peennellopeee whattssss happenningggg?" Jilly cried.

Penelope had read about volcanoes in school

and had even watched one erupt on a video her teacher had shown. The mountain they were standing on was acting a lot like the volcanoes she had seen. The mist around them was thickening and warm chocolate gas rose from a fissure at the mountain's peak. The white chocolate caps were melting. When the mountain seized again a thick lump of chocolate squirted out the top. It was only a matter of time before it would erupt.

"This is most unusual," said Sparky, bracing himself for another tremor. "We need to find a way down, fast."

"Right," said Gretel, stepping forward. "Hansel, do you remember the pretzel stairs we climbed when we were searching for Papa?"

Hansel did remember! He led them to the other side of the ridge where they could see the pop rock hill and the ice cream float boats bobbing on the fizzy blue sea. The pretzel stairs were right below.  The ground was shaking, the pop rocks popping, the mist heating up, then the earth split at their feet.  The ridge they were standing on began to crumble.

Jilly watched in horror as the pretzel stairs tumbled into the sea in an avalanche of fudge chunks. They made tidal waves that rocked the

ice cream float boats.  Pop rocks were raining down like crazy, falling into the fissure at the top of the mountain.  The friction from them popping was making the chocolate heat up faster.  The mountain rumbled, it was going to blow!

Penelope grabbed Jilly's hand as the volcano erupted and the ridge gave out beneath them. They slid over bumps, crashed through chocolate chunks and were caught up in a melted river, finally falling with a splash into the fizzy blue sea.

# Attack Of The Snow Cones

A pretzel log floated to the surface, bursting through the chocolate chunks with Jilly and Penelope clinging to it.  The chocolate mountain had melted down to nothing and was now a small hill.  Jilly and Penelope floated past capsized ice cream float boats that had sunk when the volcano erupted.  The ends of their long spoon masts stuck above the surface.  Hansel, Gretel and Sparky were nowhere in sight.

"I wonder where they are," said Jilly, looking concerned.

She kicked her feet in time with Penelope, half heartedly moving along, watching the water for signs of her friends.  A capsized ice cream float boat loomed like an island before them.  They had just about reached it when the hombre frog floated by.

"Ieeeeee-ihaaaaaaaaa!" he cried, waving Jilly's goody bag in one hand and jingling Princess Annie's ball in the other. Then he disappeared into a hole in the side of the boat.

"Come on," said Penelope, kicking harder, "don't you want to get your goody bag back?"

"Nope," Jilly replied, letting her feet drift for a moment. "I love sweets but too much of a good thing can be really bad." Penelope nodded her head in agreement. "But I did promise to get Princess Annie's ball back."

They kicked until they reached the ice cream island. A large hole had been knocked into its side. Fizzy blue water was flowing in and out of the hole washing pretzel sticks and other debris into its mouth. As they kicked closer Penelope and Jilly were caught up in the current and pulled through the opening into an underwater cavern.

The inside of the cavern was made of the ship's deck. The captain's wheel hung upside down. They could hear the drip of melting ice cream plopping into the water. They held onto the pretzel log and kicked blindly though the dark not knowing where they were going or how to get back the way they had come. Currents of warm water rushed against pools of cold melted ice cream, heating then cooling their feet as they kicked. Then something brushed against Jilly's toe.

"Aah!" she cried, pulling her foot out of the water. The pretzel log spun in a circle.

"What is it?" said Penelope, pulling her feet up too.

"Something brushed past me, I think it's still there," said Jilly, scanning the water.

"We need to keep going," Penelope replied.

They started to kick. Rings of water circled around them. The thing that had brushed against Jilly's toe was still there and it was keeping pace. Thin black shapes rose all around them poking through the dark waters before dipping beneath the surface again. It was impossible to know how many were there!

"Which way is out?" Jilly asked. But Penelope didn't know.

"Just keep kicking!" she said.

They kicked faster and as they did the long thin shapes rose and fell faster too. Then the water started to churn. Penelope and Jilly were lifted up on their pretzel raft. Tentacles waved around them glowing in the dim light. They were riding on the head of a giant gummy octopus!

The octopus was breathing deeply then blasting water out of his siphon to move forward, it was using its eight arms to steer.

"I think we are heading towards the other side of the cavern," said Penelope.

The octopus was picking up speed. It was lighter here and the fizzy water had turned a brighter shade of blue. The octopus turned bright blue too!  It slapped its tentacles down in the water as it blasted forward.  Each time it did, dozens of Swedish fish stuck to the suction cups on its arms.  The octopus gobbled them up then slapped its tentacles down again.  The cavern grew even lighter and Penelope could now see Jilly kneeling beside her.  A smooth wall of ice cream rose up in front of them.

"I think it's going to crash through!" cried Penelope.

The octopus breathed in deeply. A huge blast of water shot out its siphon and the octopus crashed through the wall.  Ice cream slid into the water.  Giant waves rose on the surface.

"Jump!" cried Penelope, as the octopus dove underwater.

Penelope and Jilly washed up on a vanilla shore, surrounded by chocolate dunes sprinkled with gummy starfish and sticky strawberry jellyfish. A long spoon stuck out of the sand. Tied to it were Sparky, Hansel and Gretel, their hands secured with licorice ropes, their mouths covered with candy wrappers. Jilly rushed over to Sparky and pulled the wrapper off his mouth.

"Look out it's a trap!" he barked, but his warning came too late.

From behind the dunes hopped the hombre frog, Princess Annie was by his side. As she tossed her golden ball, a jingling sound filled the air. Then the sand began to quiver. Behind them rose an army of snow cones that marched onto the beach. In their hands were silver tridents. They had beady eyes and angry mouths made of sprinkles and melted caramel. An icy storm cloud rose in the sky behind them.

"You!" cried Jilly, stepping closer until her nose touched princess Annie's. "You let my friends go!"

"But I thought *we* were friends," Princess Annie frowned.

"Friends don't tie people up and friends don't lie," said Jilly pointing to the hombre frog. "You were working together all the time!"

Princess Annie looked surprised. "What do you mean?"

"You let that hombre frog take your golden ball. Everywhere he hopped it jingled in his belly and turned Candy Land sour. You knew that would happen!"

"No," said Princess Annie, her eyes filling with tears, "I only wanted to show Daddy that I could be more responsible and not lose my things. The hombre frog gave me my ball back." Just then a clap of thunder rattled the dunes and broke apart the icy storm cloud.

Penelope grabbed Jilly's hand and pulled her behind the long spoon. This was just the distraction they needed. She held a finger to her lips then she untied Sparky. Jilly nodded and untied Gretel. Penelope had just loosened the licorice that held Hansel when the Evil Wizard emerged from the depths of the icy storm cloud riding his dragon.

"Now I have you, give me the golden ball!" he cried, swooping lower so he could snatch it from Princess Annie's hand. She cowered behind the hombre frog.

"Don't give it to him!" Jilly shouted, "Throw the ball to me!"

"Who are you going to trust that nasty little girl or me? Give me the ball!" demanded the Evil Wizard. He held out his hand.

Silently, Hansel stooped down and scooped

up a handful of the vanilla beach and pressed it into a ball. He handed it to Jilly and then started making another. Jilly smiled. Soon they all had ice cream snowballs. Hansel held up three fingers putting each down slowly, *one, two three!* Jilly, Penelope, Hansel and Gretel threw their snowballs at the Evil Wizard at the same time knocking him off his dragon. He slid across the frosty beach spinning slowly to a stop, a gummy starfish stuck to his head.

"Get them!" the Evil Wizard commanded, waving his hand in the air.

The snow cone army began to advance on Jilly and her friends. Hansel made snowballs as fast as he could, but there were too many snow cones and they were coming too fast. The children ran and hid behind the long handled spoon, its curved end glinting in the sunlight. Penelope grabbed Jilly's hand.

"I have an idea," she cried, "help me turn this spoon!" They grabbed the spoon's long handle and turned it until the sun reflected off the curved end. A beam of light shown down on the snow cone army melting them with its burning ray until there was nothing left but a sticky puddle.

"This is not over yet," said the Evil Wizard jumping to his feet. He ran towards Princess Annie who still held the golden ball and tried to grab it out of her hand.

"Throw it here!" Jilly cried, reaching her arms up high. But Princess Annie stood frozen. The Evil Wizard lunged for the ball. Just before he grabbed it Princess Annie threw the ball into the air. The Evil Wizard jumped to catch it, but he was too slow, the hombre frog's long pink tongue shot out and stuck to the curved side of the ball. He pulled in his tongue and swallowed the ball with a gulp. The Evil Wizard sat down hard on the frosty beach.

"It was you all the along!" accused Jilly, facing the Evil Wizard. "It was you who put a spell on Princess Annie's golden ball and you who tried to turn Candy Land sour!"

The Evil Wizard laughed. "You may have figured out my plan but it's too late to stop it! Wherever that hombre frog hops the candy will turn sour and soon, Princess Annie, your father will have to turn all of Candy Land over to me or see his realm destroyed, mwahahaha!"

A big tear slid down Princess Annie's face. Jilly took her hand. "Don't cry, we will think of something." Then Jilly's eyes grew wide, she knelt down in front of Princess Annie. "Annie, do you remember the story of the frog prince?" Annie nodded. "Remember how the spell was broken and the frog turned back into a prince when the princess kissed him?" Annie nodded again. "Well, if you kiss the hombre frog, then the spell will be broken and Candy Land will be saved." Princess Annie frowned, she didn't want to kiss a frog! "Besides, it would show your father how responsible you are," said Jilly.

Princess Annie knew Jilly was right. She took a deep breath then leaned down and kissed the hombre frog on the very tip of his sombrero. A green light filled the air spreading over the beach and the fizzy blue sea, then it sped up the mountain turning Candy Land back to normal.

"No!" cried the Evil Wizard, stamping his feet. He jumped on the back of his dragon and flew off into the bright blue cotton candy sky.

# Too Much of a Good Thing

Jilly, Penelope, Hansel, Gretel, Princess Annie and Sparky found themselves standing on the deck of an ice cream float boat.  The hombre frog was gone and in his place stood a little boy, a golden crown sparkled on his head.

"Who are you?" asked Princess Annie.

"My name is Manuel, I was turned into a frog by the Evil Wizard. I've been trying to find my way back home ever since, but I got lost."

Princess Annie smiled and took his hand. "Don't worry, I bet my father can help you."

"Do you really think so?" said Manuel.

"I know so," Princess Annie replied.

They set sail for Princess Annie's castle. While the others talked Jilly and Penelope sat down next to Sparky. Jilly put her arms around his furry neck and gave him a big hug.

"Thanks for finding us," she said, "but I think its time we went home too."

Sparky nodded, stepping back as Penelope pulled two puzzle pieces out of her pocket. She handed one to Jilly. On it was a picture of Hansel and Gretel's tree house. It had been rebuilt and the forest dripped with dark maple sugar once again. Penelope looked at hers. The picture showed a rainbow stretching over the towers of a castle.

"I guess we fixed these stories," she said, as she spoke Manuel walked over to where they stood. He held the blue spotted goody bag in his hand.

"I think this is yours," he said, handing it to Jilly. She looked at the bag then handed it back.

"No, you keep it," said Jilly, "I think I've had enough sweets for one day."

They waved goodbye to Hansel, Gretel, Princess Annie and Manuel then Jilly fitted her puzzle piece into the one Penelope held, there was a flash of light and they were gone.

When the light faded Penelope and Jilly were standing in the secret room at the library. It was no longer filled with melted chocolate, in fact it wasn't filled with anything at all. Instead, they found a note tacked to the door, it said:

Peter Piper picked a peck of pickled pirates, how many pirates did Peter Piper pick?

"What do you think that means?" asked Jilly.

"I have no idea," Penelope replied, shrugging her shoulders, "but I bet we're going to find out."

"I sure hope it involves some pirate booty," said Jilly.

"I know where we can get some right, now!" laughed Penelope, slipping through the secret door. "Come on *ye landlubber,* I bet mom is waiting!"

"*Yo, ho, ho!*" Jilly cried, chasing Penelope down the long corridor.

The End

The Great Story World

Mix-Up

Continues...

# The Boy Who Cried Sea Monster

Join Penelope and Jilly as they head to the beach in their first ever out-of-the-library Story World adventure where "fun in the sun" is about to take a turn for the worst.

When a sea monster threatens the beach goers Penelope and Jilly have to find a new way to get to Story World. With the help of Peter Piper, the tongue twister champion, a band of rogue pirates and a misguided boy who yells for help at all the wrong times Penelope and Jilly will have their hands full as they try to discover how each of their new friends fits in, and how their unique talents can help scare off the sea monster lurking just off shore.

Everybody is talking about Penelope and Jilly...

*"The Great Story World Mix-Up is a unique twist on the classic tales. The authors use their 'sparkly' imagination to draw the reader in and leave them wanting more! I can't wait to see what happens next!" -Melissa Martin, Educator*

*"Finally, something refreshing and new is out there!"*
*-Helen Riesgraf, Upstate, NY*

*"The book was absolutely, positively fantastic. I loved it so much. It was probably the best book I ever read. And I've got a name for the wizard, Oswald!"*
*-2ʳᵈ Grade Student*

*"I love your books, cool website too!"*
*-2ʳᵈ Grade Student*

*"I love the concept, the characters and the writing. You and the girls did an amazing job."*
*—Laura Kelly, Educator*

*"It looks like it will be a popular series and I LOVE the illustrations!" -Laura, UK*

About the authors...

Laura Hill is the author of several novels and has penned numerous documentaries. She loves the beach, being with her family and funny looking pug dogs.

Kayla Timpanaro is a fabulous artist and natural comedian. Besides authoring GSWMU books she is our resident tech guru, editing movies and creating web pages. When she is not creating you may find her dancing in lush productions on stage or devouring a good book.

Ava Timpanaro is an inspired actress and dancer with an amazing flair for fashion. When she is not coming up with story ideas and illustrations she is creating designs for the boutiques she plans to open in New York and Paris. An animal advocate, she loves speaking to other children about her experiences.

The Great Story
World Mix-Up
is on the web...


Please visit us at

www.greatstoryworldmixup.com

OR

www.gswmu.com

Enjoy our books, games, Big Ideas and teacher's
resources.


We would love to hear from you!

Made in the USA
Charleston, SC
15 March 2014